Maisy's Chinese New Year

Lucy Cousins

WALKER BOOKS

AND SUBSIDIARIES

LONDON · BOSTON · SYDNEY · AUCKLAND

Tomorrow is Chinese New Year.
Maisy sweeps and tidies
the house to get it ready!

Then, Maisy visits a market to buy food, decorations and lovely new clothes.

Red is a lucky colour.
What red things can you see?

At home, Maisy waits for her first guest.

Who's that knocking at the door?

It's Tiger! She has come home to celebrate. Hooray!

Tallulah, Charley and Cyril arrive next.
"Welcome home, Tiger!" they all say.

Tiger has brought lots of presents and
decorations to wish everyone
happiness and luck.

They all sit at the table
to eat a delicious feast.
There are so many
things to try.

After dinner, Ostrich
and Penguin come to visit!
They give everyone lucky red
packets with money inside.

"Thank you!" says Maisy.

Maisy and her friends sit to listen to Tiger telling an exciting Chinese New Year story.

"A long, long time ago, twelve animals raced across a great river..." she begins.

"The rat won the race, but we celebrate every animal in turn.

dog

pig

rooster

monkey

goat

horse

rat

ox

tiger

rabbit

dragon

snake

And this makes up
the twelve-year
Chinese zodiac,"
Tiger explains.

The next day, everyone goes to a wonderful parade. It's so much fun!

Finally, Maisy leads her friends in a special dragon dance for good luck.